Big Cat

by Pippa Goodhart

Illustrated by Sandra Aguilar

W
FRANKLIN WATTS
LONDON•SYDNEY

Notes on the series

TIDDLERS are structured to provide support for children who are starting to read on their own. The stories may also be used for sharing with children.

Starting to read alone can be daunting. **TIDDLERS** help by listing the words in the book for a check before reading, and by providing visual support and repeating words and phrases. These books will both develop confidence and encourage reading and rereading for pleasure.

If you are reading this book with a child, here are a few suggestions:

1. Make reading fun! Choose a time to read when you and the child are relaxed and have time to share the story.
2. Talk about the story before you start reading. Look at the cover and the blurb. What might the story be about? Why might the child like it?
3. Look also at the list of words below - can the child tackle most of the words?
4. Encourage the child to retell the story, using the jumbled picture puzzle.
5. Give praise! Remember that small mistakes need not always be corrected.

Here is a list of the words in this story.

Common words:

a	not	the
and	now	then
big	said	with
is	that	

Other words:

cat	mice	squeak
fair	only	three
mouse	play	together
miaow	played	two
	six	

Big Cat played ...

... with a mouse.
"Squeak! That is not fair!"

Big Cat played ...

... with two mice.
"Squeak, squeak!
That is not fair!"

Big Cat played ...

... with three mice.
"Squeak, squeak, squeak!
That is not fair!"

13

Then six mice ...

... played with
Big Cat.
"SQUEAK!"

"Miaow!"
said Big Cat.

18

Now Big Cat and
the mice ...

... play together!

Puzzle Time

a

b

Can you find these pictures in the story?

Which pages are the
pictures from?

Turn over for answers!

Answers

The pictures come from these pages:

a. pages 8 and 9

b. pages 14 and 15

c. pages 12 and 13

d. pages 16 and 17

First published in 2010 by
Franklin Watts
338 Euston Road
London
NW1 3BH

Franklin Watts Australia
Level 17/207 Kent Street
Sydney
NSW 2000

Text © Pippa Goodhart 2010
Illustration © Sandra Aguilar 2010

The rights of Pippa Goodhart to be
identified as the author and Sandra Aguilar
as the illustrator of this Work have been
asserted in accordance with the Copyright,
Designs and Patents Act, 1988.

A CIP catalogue record for this book is
available from the British Library.

ISBN 978 0 7496 9388 6 (hbk)
ISBN 978 0 7496 9400 5 (pbk)

Series Editor: Jackie Hamley
Editor: Melanie Palmer
Series Advisor: Catherine Glavina
Series Designer: Peter Scoulding

Printed in China

Franklin Watts is a division of Hachette Children's Books,
an Hachette UK company. www.hachette.co.uk